W9-BZS-887

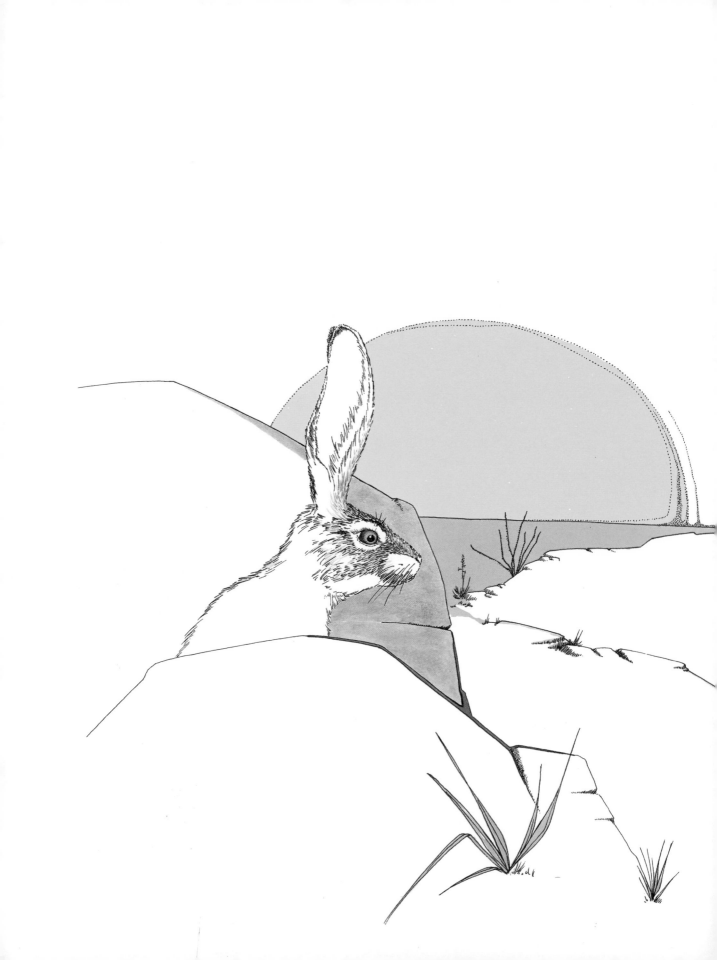

DESERT
VOICES

BY BYRD BAYLOR AND PETER PARNALL

Charles Scribner's Sons / New York

Charles Scribner's Sons
Macmillan Publishing Company
866 Third Avenue, New York, NY 10022
Collier Macmillan Canada, Inc.
Printed in the United States of America

7 9 11 13 15 17 19 20 18 16 14 12 10 8 6

Library of Congress Cataloging in Publication Data
Baylor, Byrd.   Desert Voices.
SUMMARY: Desert inhabitants describe the beauty
of their home.
[1. Deserts—Fiction. 2. Desert animals—Fiction]
I. Parnall, Peter. II. Title.
PZ7.B3435De   [Fic]   80-17061
ISBN 0-684-16712-3

To Lita Severin

PACK RAT

I run to
whatever
is shiny,
find out about
anything
new.

I sniff
a gleaming mica chip,
a feather that falls
from the sky,
a pale blue turquoise bead,
a button,
the top of an old tin can,
and the pipe
that a miner
smoked by his campfire
and left on the ground
while he slept.

I take it all.

I am a gatherer of treasure…
of leaves
and berries and roots,
mesquite beans,
sweet red summer cactus fruit,
and a piece of a clear glass bottle
turned purple by the sun.

I stay
close to home,
close to the trails I know,
close to the rocks where I was born,
close to the cholla cactus
I climb so easily.

Everything I want
is here.

In the cool evenings
I search,
darting from rock to rock,
out of sight of coyotes and owls.

I run back and forth
with my mouth full of treasures.

I go home at sunrise,
pushing
and pulling
and rolling
all the good things
back to my nest,
my pile of sticks and dirt
and cholla cactus thorns.

It holds me safe.
It hides my shining secrets
in the dust.

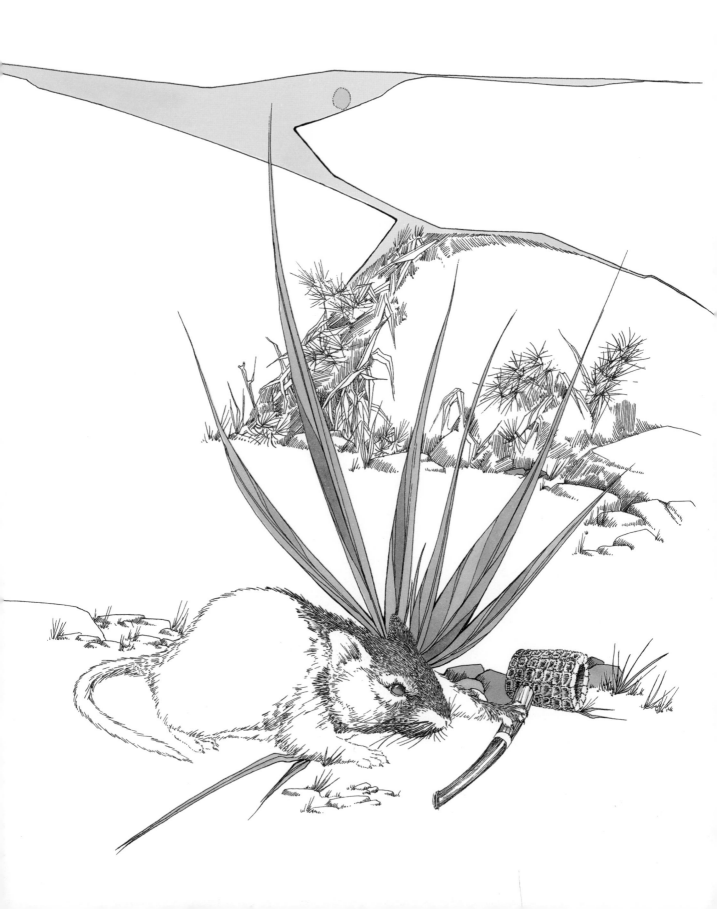

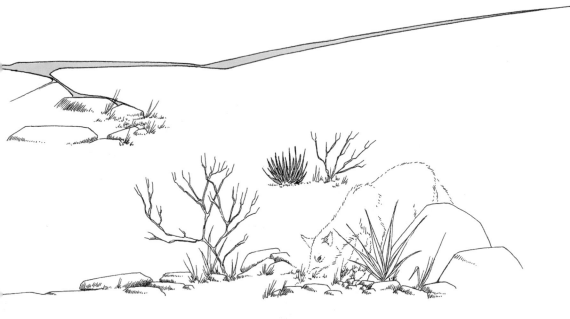

JACKRABBIT

The sudden leap,
the instant start,
the burst of speed,
knowing
when to run
and when to freeze,
how to become
a shadow
underneath
a greasewood bush…

these are things
I learned
almost at birth.

Now
I lie
on the shadow-side
of a clump of grass.
My long ears bring me
every far-off footstep,
every twig that snaps,
every rustle in the weeds.

I watch
Coyote move
from bush to bush.

I wait.
He's almost here.

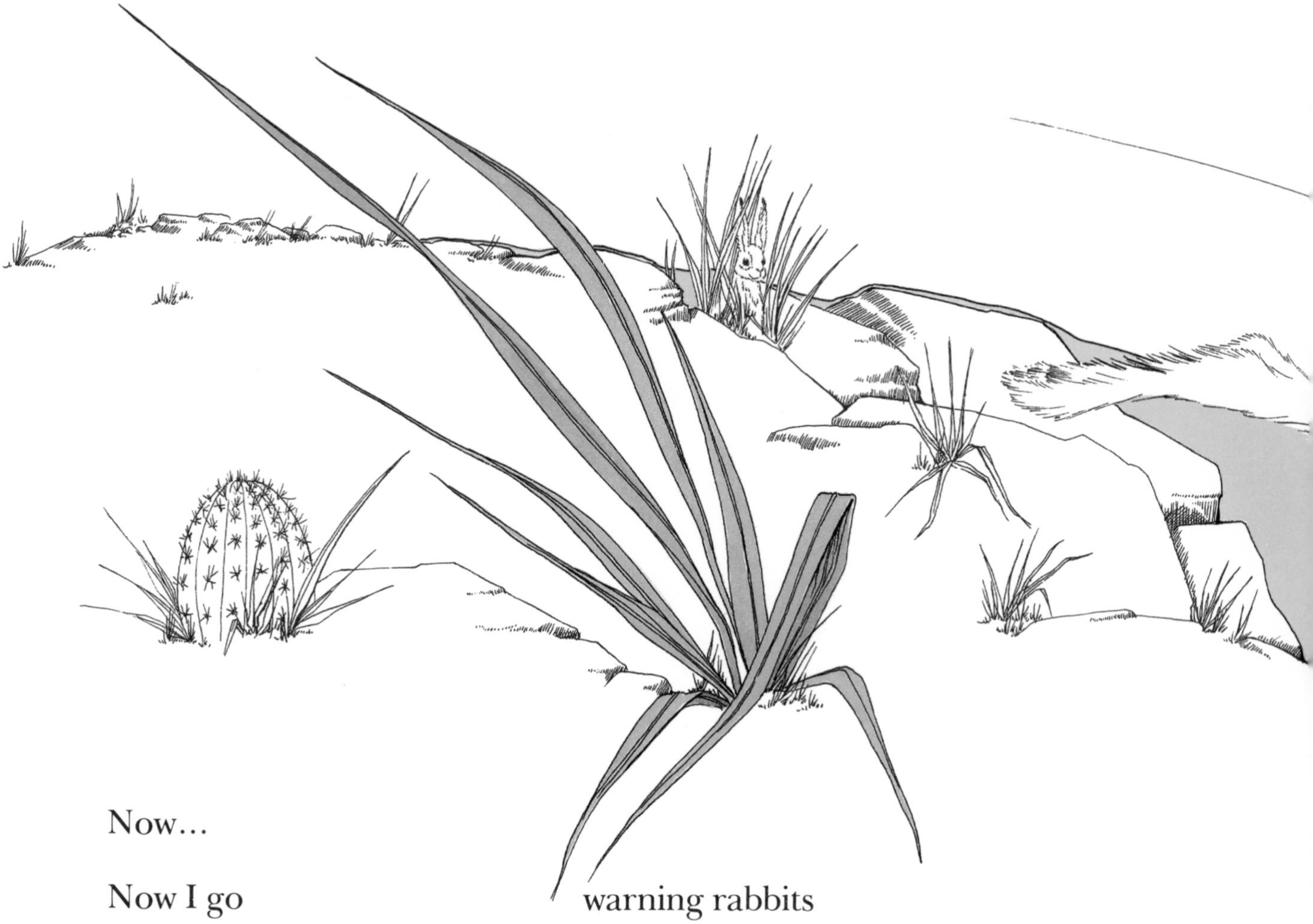

Now...

Now I go
like a zig-zag
lightning flash.
With my ears laid back,
I sail.

Jumping gullies
and bushes and rocks,
doubling back,
circling,
jumping high
to see where my enemy is,

warning rabbits
along the way,
I go.

I hardly touch
the ground.

And suddenly
I disappear.

Let Coyote stand there
sniffing
old jackrabbit trails.

Where I am now
is a
jackrabbit secret.

SPADEFOOT TOAD

Far down in the earth,
quiet as a stone,
I wait for rain.

I wait for
the first summer storm,
for wild, hard, sudden,
heavy rain
that pounds the land
above me
and calls me from
my hiding place.

Now
is the time
to dig through darkness
up to the wet
shining world.

Now is the time
for loud toad voices
to sing.

Our sound is everywhere.
It lasts all night,
rising from every puddle,
filling the air
with toad joy.

Tonight we lay our eggs.

Our tadpoles
have to grow
their new toad bodies
before the shallow pools
dry up
and turn to sand,
before
we dig our way
back down
into the earth.

The new ones
of our kind
dig, too.

They know
where to go.

They know
how to wait.

And on some rainy dawn,
they'll know
to dig straight
up.

They'll feel the rain.
They'll sing
as I sing now.

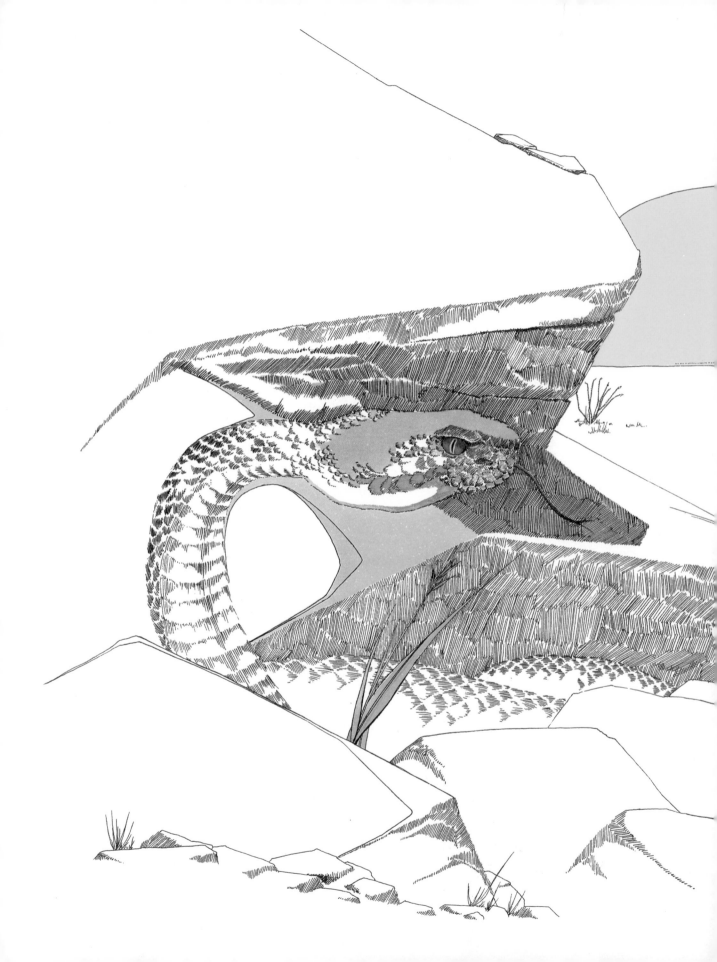

RATTLESNAKE

I move so flat against
the earth
that I know all
its mysteries.

I understand
the way sun
clings to rocks
after the sun is gone.

I understand
the long cold shadows
that wrap themselves
around me
and slow my blood
and call me back
into the earth.

On the south side of
a rocky slope
where sun can warm
my hiding place,
I wait for the cold
that draws me into
sleep.

I understand
waking
in spring,
still cold,
hardly moving,
seeking warmth,
seeking food,
going from darkness
to light.

I understand
the shedding
of old skin
and the tenderness
of my new soft shining
self
flowing
smooth as water
over sand.

I understand
the sudden strike,
the death I hold
behind my fangs.

Wherever I go
I cast
a shadow of fear.

CACTUS WREN

On the hottest
summer afternoons
when desert creatures
look for shade
and stay close to the earth
and keep their voices
low

I sit high on a cactus
and fling
my loud ringing trill
out to the sun…

over and over
again.

My home is
in a cholla cactus.
I won't live
where cactus doesn't grow
because I know
the only safe place
for a nest

is a stickery branch
in a cactus thicket.

I like thorns
in all directions.

At the entrance
of my nest
I pile more cactus.
I peck off the spines
where I go
in and out.

It is so good a nest
that when we leave it
other creatures
will move in —
a family of crickets
or a cactus-climbing mouse.

But now
it holds
six small brown birds

and me.

DESERT TORTOISE

I am the *old* one here.

Mice
and snakes
and deer
and butterflies
and badgers
come and go.
Centipedes
and eagles
come and go.

But tortoises
grow old
and *stay*.

Our lives stretch out.

I cross
the same arroyo
that I crossed
when I was young,
returning to
the same safe den
to sleep through
winter's cold.
Each spring,
I warm myself
in the same sun,
search for the same
long tender blades
of green,
and taste the same
ripe juicy cactus fruit.

I know
the slow
sure way
my world
repeats itself.
I know
how I fit in.

My shell still shows
the toothmarks
where a wildcat
thought he had me
long ago.
He didn't know
that I was safe
beneath
the hard brown rock
he tried to bite.

I trust that shell.
I move
at my own speed.

This
is a good place
for an old tortoise
to walk.

BUZZARD

I am a bird of silence.
I do not sing at dawn
or call out to my mate
across the sky.

Up on the cliff where we roost,
wind is the only sound.
I let it speak
for me.

All day
I ride on waves
of hot dry desert air,
on lifting currents
of heat,
circling without effort,
wheeling
soaring
gliding
drifting

upward.

I move with my large wings
set to the wind.

Beautiful in the sky,
I follow death.

High over the world,
I watch.

Across valleys and canyons
and wide flat desert land,
others of my kind
are watching, too.

If one of us drops down,
another follows,
and another...
and from far away,
still others come.

We kill nothing,
harm nothing alive.

I only take what is waste.

When I go
I leave nothing
but bones.

LIZARD

When my mother laid her eggs
she looked for sand
that was just right.
It had to be damp
and it had to be warmed
all day by sun.

Down in that sand
she buried her eggs.

When she left,
she didn't come back.
There wasn't any need to.
Sand and sun
are mother enough
for lizards.

I dug my way
to sunlight.
It didn't take me long
to flick my tongue
and catch a gnat
and learn
that when the sun goes down
you can be warm
beneath a little mound
of sand.

It didn't take me long
to learn
the way
a lizard runs—
just a flash of speed
across the sand,
almost too fast
to be a shape.

Now
the hotter the sun,
the better I like it.
The rougher the country,
the faster I run.

When I rest,
looking out over
the world
from a rock,
I show
the bright blue shining
color of my underside.
I seem to be made
of earth
and sky.

But then
I run again
and I'm nothing
but a blur
in the hot white sun.

COYOTE

I may live
hungry.
I may live
on the run.
I may be
a wanderer
and a trickster
and one
who'll try
anything

and a lot too nosy
for my own good

and a lot
too restless, too.

But I'm going to
make it—
no matter what.

I'll eat anything,
sleep anywhere,
run any distance,
dig for water
if I have to
because
I'm going to
survive
in this dry
rocky land…

and while I'm
doing it,
I'm going to
sing
about it.

I sing about cold,
and traps,
and traveling on,
and new soft pups
in a sandy den,
and rabbit hunts,
and the smell of rain.

I sing
for a wandering
coyote band
over there
across the hills,
telling them
coyote things,

saying
We're here
We're here
Alive
In the moonlight.

DESERT PERSON

Like any desert creature,
I build my own
safe shelter
with what the desert
gives.

I make thick walls
of mud and straw.
With my own hands
I shape the earth
into a house.

But when I say,
"This is my home,"
another desert person
always knows
that I don't mean
the *house*.

I mean
the farthest mountain
I can see.

I mean
sunsets
that fill the whole sky
and the colors
of the cliffs
and all their silences
and shadows.

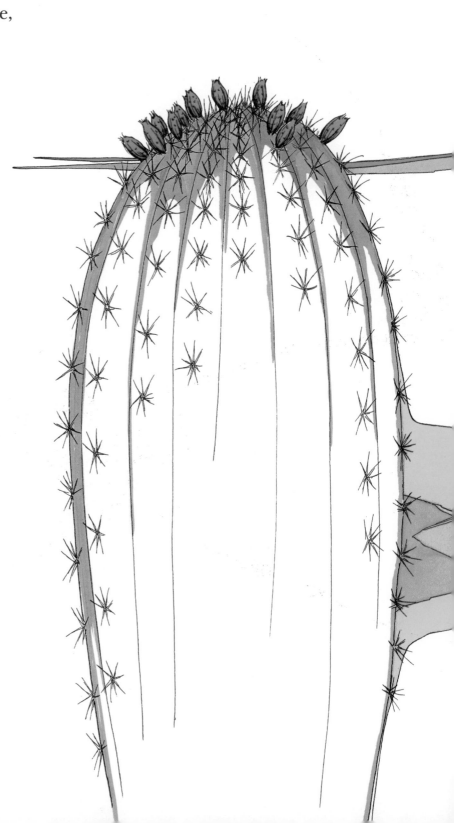

I mean
the *desert*
is my home.

Byrd Baylor and Peter Parnall
have collaborated on three Calde-
cott Honor books: *The Desert Is
Theirs; Hawk, I'm Your Brother;* and
The Way To Start a Day.

Byrd Baylor lives in the South-
west. Her eloquent lyric prose
reflects a philosophy as special
and lovely as the lands she writes
about. For her it is the spirit—not
material things—that is necessary
for personal development. "Once
you make that decision, your
whole life opens up and you begin
to know what matters and what
doesn't."

Peter Parnall lives on a farm in
Maine with his wife and two chil-
dren. His drawings have been
described as stunning, glittering
and breathtaking. When he draws
the animal world, he has an
uncanny ability to portray that
world as the animals themselves
might experience it.